Meet the ponies and get a sneak peek of the new *Pony Friends Forever* book, featuring Gizmo, Daisy and Tonto, at

www.PonyFriendsForever.com

Pony Surprise

PAULINE BURGESS

First published in 2014
by Blackstaff Press
4D Weavers Court
Linfield Road
Belfast BT12 5GH

With the assistance of
The Arts Council of Northern Ireland

Supported by
The National Lottery®
through the Arts Council of Northern Ireland

arts council of Northern Ireland

Cover design by Anne Glenn Design
Cover and internal photographs by www.prime-photography.com

Typeset by KT Designs, St Helens, England
Printed in Berwick upon Tweed by Martins the Printers

A CIP catalogue record for this book is available from
the British Library

ISBN 978 0 85640 936 3

www.blackstaffpress.com
www.ponyfriendsforever.com

For Shane, Conor
and Mark,
my very first readers.

W elcome to the Pony Palace and the second book in the *Pony Friends Forever* series. I have loved ponies since I was a little girl and now my daughter Emma loves them too. Though the people in my stories are fictional, all the horses and ponies in this series are real and living at Lessans' Riding Stables near Saintfield, County Down, where Emma and her pals ride every week.

In *Pony Surprise* you'll meet three of my favourite ponies – Skippy, Parsley and Rupert. I hope you enjoy reading their tales of fun, friendship and special surprises. Maybe, just maybe, you'll find your new PFFs – Pony Friends Forever!

Pauline

OUTDOOR ARENA

YAR

INDOOR ARENA

NOSEBAG CAFE

STABLES

OUTDOOR SEATING AREA

PONY PALACE

STABLES

CAR PARK

ACK ROOM
& OFFICE

Chapter One

SKIPPY

Okay, so I know I go too fast from time to time, but the kids love it – I *know* they do! Our owner, Kate, is cross with me again, though, so I suppose I'll have to take it easy for a while. She gave me one of her talks last night after all the kids left.

'Skippy, you know you can't just go into a canter like that. Some of the children haven't got full control over a pony like you yet. Slow down and follow instructions, or you won't be allowed out on any more rides!'

She was brushing my grey coat down and tutting at me at the same time.

'You're not a racehorse, Skippy! Gentle walks and trots, that's all you need to do in the beginners' ride. Okay?'

She gave me a pat on the shoulder to show that she wasn't being mean. Kate never likes to leave our stables without letting us know that she's still our friend. She took one last look at me before she left and I knew she was melting already.

I love it here at the Pony Palace, but I'm a horse – I'm supposed to run like the wind! I don't need a grown-up to steer me around the arena fifty times a day, and I really don't like those handlers pulling at my bridle. Just let me get on with it, that's what I say! Well, I don't actually *say* it, obviously. I just whinny and snort a bit and shake my head a lot when I'm not happy.

Saturdays are good though – that's when Ben comes for his lesson. He knows a thing or two about pushing me into a fast trot. There's no hanging around with Ben!

'Come on, girl,' he always says. 'Let's go faster. *Faster*!'

His mum lets him
ride on his own, too.
She's not pushing me
and pulling me like
some of the other
parents, no way!
Mrs Corrigan goes
up to the Nosebag
Café, drinks her

coffee and watches and waves through the big
window overlooking the arena.

'Come on, Skippy, let's show them!'
Ben shouts today at the beginning of our ride.
We trot past the other ponies and he screams
with delight. We usually manage to get one
clear round before Kate shouts out and
scolds us both. She's told Ben that he won't be
allowed back if he doesn't do as he's asked,
but when Kate's not looking Ben lowers
his head towards my ear and has a good
giggle. I saw Kate talking to his mum

about it at the end of his last lesson.

'He needs to listen to what I say, or he'll fall off and hurt himself. He's unsettling the other riders too,' she told Mrs Corrigan.

Ben's mum didn't know what to say. She just mumbled something about Ben's dad not being around and how much he looks forward to his riding lesson and how she doesn't want to spoil it for him.

'I understand that,' Kate answered. 'I'm sorry that things are hard for Ben at the minute. Horses can be really healing for children when they're going through something difficult, and I'd hate for Ben not to come back. But I have to think of his safety and the safety of the other riders.'

But when his mum tried to talk to him about it, Ben just rolled his eyes and gave me a hug.

'Grown-ups are always complaining about something, Skippy. That's why I like you –

you understand that I just want to have fun! I wish you were mine, and I could bring you home and ride on you every single day. I wish I could ride off over those big hills and disappear.'

I do too, Ben. But then again, I might miss all my friends here at the Pony Palace. Some of them are grumpy, yes, and some are downright annoying, but they're still the ponies I wake up with in the mornings and bed down beside at night. Besides, we're planning a really special event for Rupert which is absolutely TOP SECRET – so I think I'll just stay exactly where I am for now!

Chapter Two

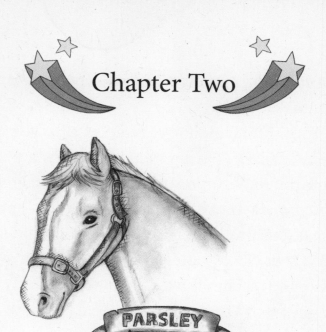

PARSLEY

I just love, love, *love* when we get to go on a hack! Sophie's riding me today and she's such a pretty little thing. She loves these leisurely strolls in the countryside just as much as I do – taking it easy, not rushing, breathing in the fresh air. Sophie's so lovely with her long, honey-coloured hair always fixed neatly into a plait, and she wears all the best riding gear too. Her new body protector is bright pink and blue, just like my browband. *Gorgeous*!

'Your browband looks so good with your chestnut mane, Parsley, *and* it matches my gear! You look so pretty today, girl. Kate looks after you all so well. She says I can come and help the beginners when I'm a little bit older. Won't that be so cool?'

Sophie reaches down and pats me gently. She says that I'm just her cup of tea. I think that means she likes me.

'Some of the other ponies are just way too frisky, Parsley – not like you. A lady like you would never misbehave! Oh, did I tell you that Mum arranged for some of my friends to come over to my house to watch a movie later? We're going to order pizza too. We'll have so much fun! I just hope they don't mess around with my things. Mum hates it when my room's untidy,' she says.

I like to listen to her just chatting away.

She tells me all about her life and school and things, but she never seems to mention friends, so I'm glad to hear that she's got pals coming over.

Her mum's riding ahead on Olga. I'm *always* at the back of the ride. A ladylike mare like me doesn't want anyone hanging around at her rear end! We pull out of the lane and turn right on to Monlough Road. There's never much traffic along here, but all the ponies keep well in to the side of the road, just in case. Kate's assistant, Jenny, is at the front of the hack leading the way. I hope she'll take us up past the lake because it always smells really nice and fresh up there. At this time of year the leaves are just changing colour and the countryside is a kaleidoscope of colours; browns, reds, coppers. It's beautiful!

Kate brought me to the Pony Palace just over a year ago and I really love it around here. Of course it's not really a palace – just

lots of stables and a riding school – but Kate says it's a really unique, special place. There's a little village nearby called Saintfield where she buys all our food and tack and things. Sophie lives in the village, and she's always telling me about her favourite shop on the main street that sells
dresses and hair
bands and shoes in
lots of shiny colours.
I'd love to see them
– horseshoes are so
boring compared
to human shoes. We're not allowed into the village because of all the traffic, but if I could, I'd sneak into Saintfield and get myself the sparkliest, most colourful shoes I could possibly find!

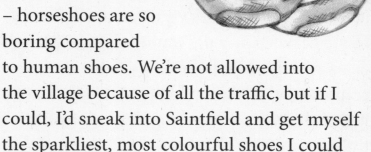

We head in the direction of the lake, just as I'd hoped. Rupert's right in front of me, plodding along as usual like he just couldn't be bothered. The rest of us ponies are keeping a very special secret from Rupert, though, and when he finds out it just *might* put a smile on his face. Jenny tells the children and adults to dismount and tie us to the fence around the little car park. Mums and dads and kids take out picnic bags and baskets, but not before giving us a few treats first. Sophie's mum is talking on her mobile phone as soon as she gets off her horse. I can see Sophie rolling her eyes.

'You wait here, Parsley. I won't be long,' she says. And she isn't. Her mum has to make another important phone call, so Sophie sits down on the ground beside me and has her picnic. Mrs Walker is a very important person, apparently. She's in charge of some big business in Belfast, so she doesn't have a lot of free time to spend with Sophie.

'Look at the lake today, Parsley. It's so clear I can see my own reflection.' She's right – the lake is crystal clear, but the face I can see reflected in the water is not a happy one. I see a lonely little girl, and I wish I could do something to make her feel better. Maybe having friends over will cheer her up. Maybe Sophie's mum will get off her mobile phone long enough to spend some time with her daughter. Just maybe.

Chapter Three

RUPERT

Here they come, running and squealing with my saddle and bridle. The kids around here are so noisy sometimes it makes my ears hurt, and they can't seem to do anything right. Honestly – it takes at least three of them to get my bit into my mouth. And when it comes to tying my girth – please! I have to squeeze my tummy in until I can hardly breathe!

It must be nearly time for me to retire. I've been working here at the Pony Palace for longer than I can remember and if I have to listen to one more 'Trot on, Rupert' I think I'll … well, neigh my head off! And I hate the way they get me mixed up with Parsley just because we're both chestnut with white-striped faces. Haven't they noticed her pink and blue browband? The white sock on her hind leg? *My* funky forelock? Plus there is the little matter of me being a boy!

'Come on, Rupert. Squeeze that belly in,' Jamie tells me.

He's underneath me reaching for the girth strap. That boy never stops smiling and joking around – he really should try being a bit more serious every so often. And that hair of his needs a good cut. It looks so goofy, flopping all over the place like that.

'That's it, Rupert. We're ready to rock and

roll. You going to do some jumps for me today?'

'Do I have a choice?' I think to myself with a snort.

Jamie is in the older ride. He's been coming  here for about two years so Kate moved him up to the third level. He's really keen on showjumping and keeps going on about something called the Olympics and 'going for gold.' Honestly, the boy's head is in the clouds!

He leads me towards the outdoor arena where Kate has laid out six sets of jumps. Barney, Tonto and Biscuit are the other ponies joining us today. I make sure to steer well clear of Barney – he's a right kicker, that one.

'Hi Jamie. All set?' Kate asks.

Jamie beams at her the way he does at everyone.

'You might need to up your tempo a bit today, Jamie,' she tells him. 'You know how Rupert can be stubborn and likes to take things easy – just be firm with him and he'll do what he's told. You don't want to lose time going around the school.'

'Great,' I think to myself. 'Just when I was looking for an easy ride!'

'How's your granddad, Jamie?' Kate asks him gently.

'Not so good today. Sometimes he feels a little better and he can sit up in bed and have a chat, but over the past few days he's been very weak. Mum says I should leave him to rest. It's a pity though – he loves to hear about my lessons.'

'Your mum's probably right, Jamie. But let's do a really good round today without cutting any corners, and then you'll be able to tell him all about it when he picks up again.'

She pats him on the arm and goes to sort out one of the other riders. Kate's nice like that – she always tries to cheer the kids up when they're down. Jamie's granddad used to ride apparently, but now he's got some kind of sickness that makes him feel really tired. I sort of feel sorry for Jamie when he talks about it, and I'm glad that our rides make him feel better, but I'd still rather be in my stable having a nice rest.

'Come on, Rupert. Walk on,' he says and squeezes his heels into my side – I stroll forward.

'No, Rupert, faster. Into trot. Come on!'

He's kicking me gently now, but I just can't summon up the energy.

'You have to show him who's boss, Jamie,' Kate calls out. 'Give him a couple of good, hard kicks – that should get him going.'

'*Okay*, okay!' I think, 'I'll pick up the pace!'

I gather speed and begin to canter around the
arena. I clear the first jump easily and steady
myself for the next one. I race towards the
cross jump but I'm feeling so fed up and tired
that I dip my head as I glide over the bars.
Jamie flies right over my head and onto the
ground with a thud. I feel guilty straight away.

'Jamie. *Jamie*!' Kate shouts.

But Jamie doesn't move. What on earth
have I done?

Chapter Four

SKIPPY

'I'm so glad I could see you today, Skippy. Mum wasn't sure if she could afford my lesson today – she doesn't get paid until the end of the month.'

Ben's lesson is over and we're in the stable together. Kate said he could stay after the ride and groom me, as a reward for being well behaved today. I love being body brushed and cleaned when my skin is warm, and Ben seems to really like doing this. He spends ages sponging me down nice and gently.

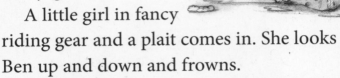

'I had to take it easy on you today, Skippy. Mum said she wouldn't let me come back if I tried to canter again. Sorry, girl.'

A little girl in fancy riding gear and a plait comes in. She looks Ben up and down and frowns.

'I can't find Parsley's dandy brush. Have you taken it?' she asks haughtily.

'No, I haven't!' Ben replies. 'This one's Skippy's. I don't go around stealing, you know.'

She stares at him. Poor Ben – he's wearing torn jeans and an old T-shirt while Little Miss stands there with her arms folded in her striped designer polo shirt and body protector.

'I didn't say you stole it,' she says, and

her bottom lip seems to quiver a bit. 'I just wondered if you'd seen it.'

'Well, I haven't. And I'm busy.'

Ben turns his back on her and starts untangling my mane. The girl marches out of the stables and goes straight up to Kate. Telling tales, no doubt!

'Stupid girl,' Ben mumbles under his breath. 'Who does she think she is?'

He starts combing my mane as if he's sandpapering a wall, not gently like he did before. The girl has obviously annoyed him.

'I'm a better rider than she is anyway. She's way too scared to even break into a trot. Proper scaredy custard.'

'Ouch! Go easy there,' I whinny.

'Rich kids!' Ben mutters.

I wish I could tell him to forget about it. Ben's much more fun when he's happy. I've never seen him this grumpy before, not even when his dad left to go and live in England.

'Ben, could I have a word?'

It's Kate. Her flame-red hair is pinned up under a riding hat and she looks tired.

'Everything okay, Ben?' she asks.

'Yeah, why?'

'Sophie appears to have lost a dandy brush. Have you seen it?'

'No, I haven't and I've already told her I haven't taken her stupid brush. She thinks I'm a thief!'

'I'm sure she doesn't, Ben. She was just wondering if you'd seen it – she wasn't accusing you of anything.'

'You wanna bet?' Ben mumbles.

Kate says nothing for a few minutes. She just watches Ben groom me for a bit and strokes me gently, which I can't say I object to.

'Really, Ben, Sophie's not what you think,' she says softly. 'Her mum and dad do spoil her, but she's a lonely little thing. I'm sure she'd like to make friends.'

'She shouldn't be such a snob then,'
Ben huffs.

'I'm going to ask her to come back in here
and sort things out,' Kate says. 'How about you
give her a chance to apologise?'

Ben looks up at me, his eyes clouded with
tears, and I realise this isn't just about a dandy
brush. When Sophie comes back in and
apologises he says nothing. He doesn't look at

her and he doesn't speak, and when she leaves, she looks miserable, too. Ben is so upset he doesn't even stay to finish brushing me. I feel sorry for both of them.

As soon as the coast is clear and it's just us ponies, we start planning Rupert's TOP SECRET big day. Parsley and I neigh about all the treats that will be on offer, and Biscuit and Barney join in, but I have to remind them that Rupert is not to know about any of this. Kate told us about the big event that she's got planned for Rupert and swore us all to secrecy. Old Rupert can be a bit of a grump sometimes, but we all agree that no one deserves the special day more than he does.

Chapter Five

PARSLEY

Skippy is going on about Rupert's big day again, but I'm too busy worrying about Sophie to listen. She cried for the rest of the afternoon after her argument with Ben, and I hate to see her like that. Her mum didn't notice anything was wrong when she picked her up, of course, and as usual Sophie kept it to herself.

Her movie night didn't go so well either,

the poor thing – only one girl turned up. The girls in her class don't seem to like her very much. They're probably just jealous of all her nice things. The truth is that Sophie is the sweetest little girl when you get the chance to know her. She's just not very good at making friends, and I do wish she'd learn not to frown so much.

Ben comes in later with the dandy brush. He's muttering to himself about finding it on the floor in the tack room, and how Sophie shouldn't have jumped to 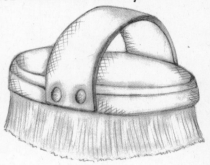 conclusions. I'm still cross at him for upsetting my Sophie, but he comes over and strokes me, which I must admit I quite like. He tells me how glossy I look, but I know that already – Sophie did a great job on me. She knows I always like to look my best.

Kate pops in and tells Ben it's time to go home.

'Feeling better?' she asks.

He nods but doesn't say anything. The boy has obviously lost his tongue!

'I just don't like people looking down at me,' he says eventually. 'That's why I was cross with her.'

'I understand, Ben, but you know what they say – you shouldn't judge a book by its cover. Maybe you should try getting to know Sophie a bit better. Come along to the hack tomorrow and ride with her. It's about time you started spending more time with the other riders anyway. Humans can be friendly too, you know, not just horses,' she laughs.

'You know Mum can't afford to send me on the hack tomorrow,' Ben mutters.

'Your mum doesn't have to pay – *you* do,' Kate explains. 'You can help me tack up all the horses for the ride and then put them back in their stables afterwards. There'll be mucking out too, of course. Do we have a deal?'

'Deal.'

He smiles, but when he walks away he has his head down again. He doesn't even say thank you. Honestly, young people nowadays – where *do* they get their manners from?

One thing is for sure, if Kate thinks I'm going to gallop along after Skippy on the hack tomorrow, she can think again. I take a ride at my own pace and I *don't* fancy trying to keep up with that flying machine!

Besides, Sophie and Ben have nothing in common. What on earth will they have to talk about? Kate means well, but if you ask me, sometimes she should just leave well enough alone.

'Here you go, Parsley. Time for dinner,'

she says, throwing in some haylage. 'Big ride tomorrow, girl. You'll need lots of energy.'

'You think?' I whinny. Sorry, Kate, but I'll be right at the back where I like to be, taking my time and riding like the lady I am!

'Have you and Skippy been whispering about the big day again?' she asks me.

'Just a bit,' I snort back. 'Have you bought the lovely ribbons and bows yet?'

It's almost as if she understands, because she tells me how gorgeous I'm going to look and how we'll all get an extra special grooming on the morning of the TOP SECRET big day. Oh, I do love it when we have special events at the Pony Palace.

ryone gets so excited and it's almost like
ere's magic in the air. There's just over a
week to go now and Sophie and I will be as
pretty as a picture!

Chapter Six

RUPERT

I didn't mean for Jamie to get injured, honestly – I was just fed up being made to go faster all the time. The truth is that I'm tired; tired of going fast, tired of jumping and tired of being told what to do.

Of course, Kate was cross with me afterwards. She gave me a right telling off, and she even said I did it on purpose. She gave me that disappointed look that makes you feel y bad about yourself.

'Jamie relies on you, Rupert! His grandfather is very ill and his poor mum is run ragged looking after the family. Jamie comes here to get away from all that. You're supposed to take his mind off things and make him feel better.'

He missed his last lesson, but he's back today and I've been told to behave myself. One of the volunteers leads me towards the outside arena where Jamie's chatting to a smaller boy. Ben's his name, I think. Jamie's arm is in some kind of bandage, but he's smiling as usual.

'You'll probably be allowed to start jumping next summer,' Jamie is telling the other boy. 'Kate will want to make sure you're really in control of your pony first. Not that I had much control of Rupert last time,' he laughs. 'It was a good lesson for me – never get overconfident around a horse!'

I can't believe he's making a joke of it! I guess I'm relieved, though. He's not a bad lad, Jamie, even if he does have that big, silly smile and floppy hair. He's always kind to the younger kids, and he's probably one of the better riders here.

'Hi there, Rupert,' he says when he spots me. 'Or should I call

you Bronco Barney?'

Clearly I am *not* Bronco Barney – I am Reliable Rupert, but Jamie's little joke makes him and the other lad laugh, so I don't mind. A little girl walks over to us, and Ben suddenly goes quiet.

'Hi, I'm Sophie. Do you mind if I watch you today?' she asks Jamie.

'Sure,' he smiles, 'But if you've come to watch me fall off again you'll be disappointed. Rupert and I are the best of mates – aren't we, Rupert?'

He rubs my nose as if the fall never happened. The girl blushes and stammers something about not wanting to see him fall.

'It's okay, Sophie. I was only joking,' Jamie says. 'You usually ride Parsley, don't you?'

'Yes. We're going on a hack in a little while. I love riding through the countryside.'

'Me too. Hey, maybe I'll join you.'

Ben is silent. He seems put out, and I get the impression that he doesn't like the girl very much. Jamie mounts me and squeezes me into a trot.

'Come on, buddy. Let's see if we can get over a few jumps today without me somersaulting off you.'

Just this once I decide to do my very best. Someone as forgiving as Jamie doesn't deserve to be mucked about. I let Jamie guide me and I work with him. I glide over the bars faultlessly and keep a nice rhythm. When we're finished, Jamie gets a big round of applause from all the parents and kids who've been watching us.

'Rupert, you're a star!' he tells me. Actually, I'm not – I'm a grumpy old chestnut gelding with an attitude, but for once I feel rather special. Just for a moment, mind you. Then Jamie leads me back into the stable and I notice all the other ponies in a huddle together, like they're plotting something. They've been acting like that since last week.

Oh, let them get on with it – if they don't want to include me in their tittle-tattle, then so be it. What do I care?

Chapter Seven

SKIPPY

Wahey! The fields and hedges are a blur as Ben and I go flying through the countryside. Kate's letting us having a canter today because there are plenty of volunteers around to keep an eye on us.

'You take care now, Skippy,' she told me before we left. 'No funny business. Ben's only eight years old, remember.'

It's cold and dry today, but Ben and I can

barely feel a thing except the wind in our hair. This is the life! The lane is hard with frost and the trees are bare and still. Ben is screaming with delight, and Mrs Corrigan had a big smile on her face when she waved him off. We won't go too far, of course. Kate says we have to wait for the slowcoaches at the bottom of the lane before we turn onto the road. She's always really careful when the riders are on the road, even though there are so few cars.

'Yee hah!' Ben shouts. 'It's like the Wild West!'

Well not *exactly*, Ben – but hey, if you want to be a cowboy you go right ahead. He's in such a good mood today. He says his dad is back in touch again and might even come home to see him soon.

'Ben! Skippy! Wait up!' Kate shouts.

'Woah, girl. We have to slow down now, but what a ride.'

Ben pulls at my reins and I can hear him panting with enjoyment.

'Hiya, Ben.' Jamie says, pulling up on Rupert. Sophie and Parsley follow close behind. Rupert eyes me with disdain and snorts. He can be *such* a grump! Sometimes I wonder why we're all making such a big effort to plan his TOP SECRET surprise.

'Looks like you had a great ride,' Jamie says.

'It was brilliant! I feel so happy and free when I ride like that. Everything else just disappears.'

'I know what you mean,' Jamie smiles. 'How about you, Sophie?'

'I prefer to go a little slower than Ben,' she says shyly, smiling at Jamie but looking warily at Ben. 'But I do know what it feels like to leave the world behind and just be with your favourite horse.'

Ben nods in agreement and I'm glad. I think it's about time those two made up.

The three of us trot along the bridle path;

me and Rupert side-by-side and Parsley trailing at the back as usual. Sophie talks less than the boys, but I can tell that she's enjoying herself. It's nice to see them all starting to get along and putting their differences aside – and of course, they talk mainly about us, which makes Parsley, Rupert and I swell with pride. Yes, even Rupert!

Chapter Eight

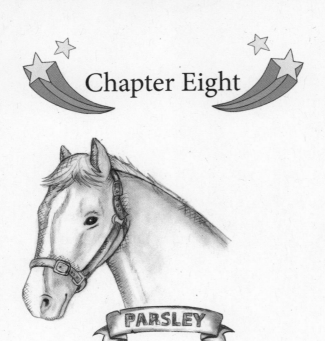

PARSLEY

I just love winter! All that extra haylage and glittery frost – what's not to like? And it's only a week or so until I get to wear sparkling bows and colourful ribbons (for Rupert's big day, of course!) which will really set off my shiny chestnut coat.

We're stopped at the lake now and the kids are talking about their plans for mid-term break. Sophie tells them she's going skiing and

Ben rolls his eyes. How rude! Rupert seems bored and is staring into the distance and Skippy's skipping around as usual wanting to get going again. Honestly – doesn't that pony understand what having a rest means?

'Here you go, Parsley. You didn't think we'd forgotten the carrots, did you?' Sophie holds her hand out flat and I munch on the crunchy carrots she offers. Delicious! She shares them around the other ponies.

'My granddad's gone back into hospital,' Jamie tells Sophie and Ben while breaking the carrots in half. 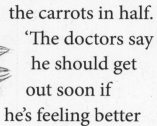 'The doctors say he should get out soon if he's feeling better after his treatment, though.'

'Imagine being in hospital for days on end. He must be so bored!' says Ben.

'It's not so bad. The doctors and nurses are really kind to him and we bring him lots of newspapers and books to read every time we visit. And my dad visits him every day and spends an hour with him just chatting about stuff.'

'My dad's in England,' Ben says unhappily. 'But when he comes back to visit I'm going to show him how well I can ride. He's never seen me ride before. He'll be amazed.' He seems to cheer up at the thought of it.

'Definitely. He'll be dead impressed,' Jamie says helpfully. 'What about you, Sophie? Are your mum and dad pleased with how your riding's coming along?'

Sophie hesitates.

'Sort of,' she says. 'But they both have really important jobs and they work a lot, so they're kind of too busy to notice. They buy me all the best riding gear though,' she adds, frowning at Ben's clothes.

'Poor little rich girl,' Ben mumbles.

'Can't you two give each other a break?' asks Jamie. 'What does it matter how much money you have? The important thing is that your families are healthy. You don't know how lucky you both are!'

He sounds cross all of a sudden, which surprises me. Nothing ever makes Jamie cross. Even Rupert looks up in astonishment.

'We're here to ride and look after the ponies and make friends,' Jamie adds, '*not* to argue and bicker.'

Sophie and Ben both hang their heads like they're ashamed. I spot Kate heading over our way, as if she senses a row.

'Come on, guys, let's get back to Pony Palace,' she says. Her nose is as red as a cherry from the cold.

'Some good riding back there, Ben. How's Parsley riding today, Sophie?'

'Great. She's always great, aren't you, Parsley?'

Of course I am, darling. I'm a princess among nags and donkeys!

'You make a good team,' Kate tells her. 'It's important for a pony and its rider to get on well together. Actually, I was wondering if you could help me out next weekend, Sophie. I need to make Pony Palace look nice and festive for the, erm … celebrations.'

Kate looks over her shoulder to see if

Rupert's listening, but he doesn't seem to have heard anything.

'I'd *love* that, Kate!' says Sophie. 'I'll bring banners and balloons and ...'

'Hey, slow down,' Kate laughs. 'You don't have to bring anything, Sophie. I've got everything we need – except help. So you're up for it then?'

'Defo!'

'What about you guys?' Kate asks the boys. 'Would you like to help out?'

'Count me in,' says Jamie.

'Me too,' Ben says quietly.

'Brilliant!' Kate says, clapping her hands together. 'Oh, and there's just one more thing. I'll need some adults to help me lay out lots of hay bales in the arena for seating. Can you ask if any of your parents are available to help?'

The kids look at each other with worried expressions. There's no way Sophie's mum

and dad will have time to lay out hay
bales – not with so much *important business*
to do on their mobile phones. And as for
Jamie and Ben's parents – what is Kate
thinking of?

Chapter Nine

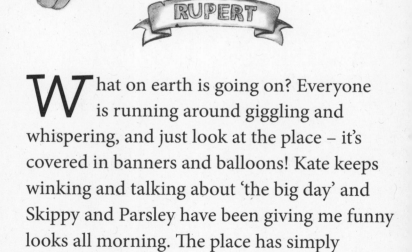

What on earth is going on? Everyone is running around giggling and whispering, and just look at the place – it's covered in banners and balloons! Kate keeps winking and talking about 'the big day' and Skippy and Parsley have been giving me funny looks all morning. The place has simply gone mad!

When Jamie arrives he has a big smile

on his face as usual.

'Hi Rupert! Look what I've got for my favourite horse – a nice juicy apple. Here you go, boy,' Jamie says.

Okay, so maybe these special events do have their perks, though I *still* don't know what this one's all about. I wish someone would tell me what's going on!

'My mum is coming along in a bit to help out with the decorations,' says Jamie. 'I couldn't believe it when she said she could spare the time, she's normally so busy looking after Granddad. I can't wait to show her some jumping. You will be a good boy, won't you?'

What does he think I am? A delinquent?

'Doesn't the place look good, Rupert?'

he says. 'Come on, I'll saddle you up and take you to the indoor arena.'

He leads me outside where Jenny is standing on a ladder putting up some kind of banner. A few parents stand around shouting instructions and helping to get it into position while others carry bunting and lights towards the arena. Kate is standing in the middle of the yard chatting to Sophie and a tall man in a smart coat. Kate is smiling and nodding a lot and Sophie is blushing bright red. The man seems very happy about whatever Kate is telling him.

'Hi Sophie!' Jamie calls over to her and waves, and they walk toward us.

'Hi Jamie. This is my dad,' she beams. 'He's come to help out today.'

'Nice to meet you, Mr Walker,' Jamie says, polite as always. Then he shakes the man's hand. 'Sophie's a great rider. She's really patient with the horses – especially Parsley.'

The man looks proudly at his daughter as Jamie speaks.

'So Kate's been telling me. I've been so busy I haven't even had the time to come and see her ride. But that's going to change. Right Sophie?' he says.

'Right, Dad,' she answers, though she doesn't look so sure.

'And who's this?' Mr Walker asks, looking at me.

'This is Rupert. He really has a mind of his own,' Jamie laughs.

'I most certainly do – and there's nothing wrong with that!' I think, and I stamp my feet just to prove it.

Just then, a green car drives up to the stables. It pulls up beside us and a woman helps a sick-looking man out of the back seat and into some kind of moving chair. He looks as pale as Skippy and the woman makes a big fuss over him, tucking a blanket around him and fixing his scarf.

'Why, that looks like Harry Hall,' Sophie's dad says, watching him. He opens his eyes wide. 'It *is* Harry Hall!' he shouts excitedly.

He walks over quickly and shakes the man's hand, telling him that he used to love watching him jump and how he was the greatest in Northern Ireland. Sophie walks shyly over to them and I can hear her dad introducing her. Jamie seems frozen to the spot. The man in the chair is looking at him and smiling, though he looks very frail. Tears roll down Jamie's face. The woman pushes the chair towards Jamie.

'We thought we'd surprise you,' she

says, and there are tears in her eyes, too. 'Your granddad really wanted to see you ride, and we know happy you are when you're here at the Pony Palace.'

Jamie gives his granddad the biggest hug ever. Then he pushes him towards me and the old man looks me over very carefully.

'So this is Rupert,' he says. 'Good strong shoulders and girth. A nice compact pony. I can see why you like him so much, Jamie. I can see why you'll miss him too.'

Miss me? Is Jamie going away somewhere? Jamie must sense my confusion, because he scratches me behind the ear and tells me not to worry, that we'll still see each other all the time. This confuses me even *more*, but then Jamie's granddad gets out of his moving chair and starts stroking me gently and I forget all about it. I can tell he's been around horses a lot. He speaks in a low voice and makes me feel calm and happy – and even a bit less grumpy. Seeing Jamie with his granddad makes me feel sort of warm inside, and I can't help but feel really pleased for both of them. Yes, that's right – grumpy old Rupert has a soft side! Goodness knows what other surprises are in store …

Chapter Ten

SKIPPY

Even though the arena is starting to look quite snazzy and everyone else is in high spirits, Ben looks really down. I can see him watching Sophie and Jamie's families drinking coffee together in the Nosebag Café, and I know what he's thinking. I nuzzle him to get his attention, hoping he wants to ride like the wind today, but he doesn't even seem to notice me.

'Come on, Ben, time to do some balance exercises,' says Kate.

Ben's in the same group as Sophie today and we're going around in the usual slow circles.

'Okay everybody – arms out like an aeroplane,' shouts Kate. 'Great! Now, reach out and touch your pony's poll. And now its tail – that's right, reach right back!'

Ben's still really glum. I just know he's fed up with warm ups and wants to take off into a canter.

'Now, stand up in your stirrups and hold the front of your saddle for the count of five.'

Oh please! Ben could do this in his sleep. Is this really necessary, Kate?

'Okay. Now we're going to practise some of those balancing exercises in trot. Ready everyone?' Kate calls. 'Whole ride in trot, please.'

So we go into trot and she makes the kids wave to the left and wave to the right, but I can hear Ben sighing above me and I decide it's time to take action. I can't just let him be down in the dumps all day! Ben's kicking me into a faster trot, and I decide there and then to take off. I go into a canter, and pretty soon I'm galloping around the indoor arena and Ben is squealing at the top of his voice. I hear Kate shouting, but I don't listen. I ride like I'm the fastest race horse in the world and I won't stop for anybody. Faster and faster I go – this is the life! The parents are standing still,

staring, and I hear some of the kids panicking
and backing out of the way but I don't care. I
feel as light as a feather and I never want
to stop!

'Skippy, stop! *Now*!'

Kate is running after me, trying to slow me
down. Begging me.

'Come on, Skippy, slow down. That's a good
girl. Take it easy,' she says, breathing hard.

Gradually, I slow my pace. 'That's my girl, come to Kate.'

She's holding on to my bridle now, hushing me, patting me on the shoulder. Finally, I stop. Ben jumps off and Kate catches him. I expect him to tell me that he had fun, that he enjoyed the ride, but he looks confused and there's fear in his eyes. Parsley shoots me *the* most disapproving look ever and Sophie dismounts and gives Ben a big hug. Mrs Corrigan puts her arm around him and leads him out of the arena, and he doesn't look back at me. Not even once.

Kate leads me back to the stables in silence. I don't understand. Ben needed cheering up and that's all I was trying to do. The big day is tomorrow and I'm beginning to wonder if I'll even be allowed to attend. I'm so confused and ashamed. I blow hard through my nostrils and snort like a hungry hippo with a toothache!

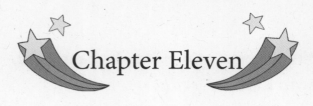

Chapter Eleven

PARSLEY

We're lined up together in the big stable; Skippy, Rupert and me. Skippy has her head hung low and she has none of her usual energy. She probably thinks Ben doesn't like her anymore. Well, it's about time she learned her lesson – Kate's been warning her about her speed for ages after all. Rupert, on the other hand, is looking unusually cheerful. I'm beginning to think he's got a softer side after all – I noticed him nuzzling Jamie earlier after his granddad left.

'Hi Parsley, I just popped in to say goodbye. What an afternoon. Did you see my dad? I can't believe he came!'

Sophie seems really excited.

'Kate's invited all our parents to the special ceremony tomorrow so I hope, hope, *hope* Mum and Dad can both make it. It would be so cool to have everyone together for the big day.'

I'm busy wondering if Rupert has figured out that it's *his* big day when Jamie walks in. Rupert reaches his head out towards him and nuzzles him.

'Hi Sophie. Today was a bit of a turn up, wasn't it?' Jamie says.

'It sure was,' Sophie answers. 'First my dad and then your granddad! It's just a pity Ben's dad couldn't be there.'

'He seemed really down in the dumps

today, didn't he? And then when Skippy took off like that, he looked so frightened.'

Poor Skippy flinches beside me.

'I really hope he's okay. I was so worried,' she says quietly, and all of a sudden I'm very proud of my little Sophie. I just *knew* there was a big well of kindness in there somewhere.

'Do you think your granddad will make it to the ceremony tomorrow?' Sophie asks Jamie.

'I don't know. Today really tired him out, so we'll have to wait and see. Kate says she'll light the big heater in the viewing gallery and help make him as comfortable as possible, so who knows?'

'I hope he can come. It's going to be brilliant! The arena looks so beautiful now with all the decorations, and Kate said there'll be pony prizes too,' Sophie says excitedly. 'I'm going to make sure Parsley's shining like a new conker!'

'You really love her don't you?' Jamie says.

'She's my favourite horse in the whole world. Mum and Dad actually offered to buy her for me, but what's the point in that? I'd miss the fun of coming *here*!'

My ears prick up at this. Imagine being with my Sophie every day! I would be so clean I'd sparkle, *and* I'd have all the best gear. But then again, I'd be away from the other horses, and let's face it, we do understand each other. I don't think I could imagine living anywhere other than the Pony Palace.

'At least when I come here someone has to come with me,' Sophie explains. 'That way Mum and Dad have to leave work behind and spend some time with me. And besides …

I get to see you and Ben and all the other riders.' She smiles. 'The Pony Palace has taught me a lot about making friends.'

I reach my head out to Sophie and nicker softly to tell her how proud I am. I'm so happy that things are on the up for her. She's finally made some real friends, and I can see that her parents really love her, even though they don't always have the time to show it.

Speaking of love, I think we ponies had better cheer Skippy up a bit. Rupert's really good at that kind of thing, actually. He gives the best advice – probably because he's been at the Pony Palace longer than anyone else. I hope he'll have a word with Skippy tonight. We can't have her down in the dumps with the big day just round the corner!

Chapter Twelve

RUPERT

Usually I hate big, fussy events, but I have to say that the arena looks *fantastic* today. It's Sunday and the place is buzzing, and even I can't help but get into the cheerful spirit that's swirling around here. The viewing gallery is full of mums and dads and we ride into the arena to a big round of applause.

'That's it, Rupert. Walk tall and proud!' Jamie says, which is a bit difficult when you've got ribbons sticking out of your saddle.

Jamie's granddad's here again, wrapped up in a warm blanket in his moving chair. He's got a little more colour in his cheeks today, so I think he must be feeling a bit better.

Jamie's beaming from ear to ear. Kate has asked all the junior riders to line up here today for some kind of special prize-giving. There are ponies and cobs and riders of all ages.

'Good afternoon, ladies, gentlemen and children,' Kate says. She's speaking into something black and shiny that makes her voice boom out across the crowd.

'I am really pleased that so many of you could make it here today to see your children on horseback,' she says. 'I know that you all have very busy schedules, and the boys and girls and I really appreciate you coming. Today is a very big day in the history of the

Pony Palace, but I don't want to give the surprise away just yet!'

She smiles at the adults and gives the kids a big thumbs-up. Jenny, her assistant, is standing beside her with a box of brightly coloured packages. Jamie waves at his granddad who's sitting beside Mr and Mrs Walker. His granddad smiles and waves back and although Sophie's dad is gabbling away in his ear, I can tell that Mr Hall is really just concentrating on Jamie.

'First of all, I would like to award some prizes,' Kate goes on. 'Our riders have worked hard all year. There have been tears and laughter, clear jumps and occasional falls, progress and mistakes – but they've come back week after week to try it all again. I'm proud of each and every one of them.'

Kate smiles and there's a big round of applause from the audience.

'My first prize today is for dressage,' she

announces and hands out a rosette and one of the packages to one of the older girls. Then she gives out prizes for rising trots, balancing, jumping – all kinds of things. Then she announces Sophie's name for 'best care taken with her pony', and Parsley and Sophie ride forward and get a rosette and a present each. Parsley looks like the cat that's got the cream. That mare is so vain – though I have to admit, she does look pretty good. Kate gives her a halved apple and she happily gobbles it up.

'My next prize is for hard work and giving extra help around the Pony Palace. The award goes to ... Ben Corrigan!'

The audience claps and Ben rides forward on Skippy to accept his award. Skippy even gets a rosette for being 'one of the most enthusiastic ponies at the Pony Palace.' What Kate *means* is that Skippy goes way too fast, but I suppose she's trying to be nice –

something I've actually started to try out myself.

Ben dismounts and receives his prize. He pats Skippy on the shoulder before he gets back on and I'm genuinely glad that they're friends again. Skippy has been even grumpier than me since they fell out, so I'm glad Ben's forgiven her. Then, just as Ben climbs back on there's a loud whistle from the crowd.

'Thatta boy, Ben!' someone shouts.

A man in a jacket and jeans is waving from the viewing gallery. Ben waves back and shouts 'Hi Dad!' at the top of his voice. Skippy moves closer to the viewing gallery as if to say hello.

'I'm really proud of you, Ben,' the man shouts. 'You look like a real rider!'

'I *am* a real rider, Dad!' Ben shouts back, beaming from ear to ear.

His dad smiles and sits down next to Ben's mum. Ben rides back into the line, looking happier than I've ever seen him.

'I'm so pleased for Ben,' Jamie tells me quietly. 'It looks like everyone's going to have the best day ever, Rupert.'

Kate's talking to the audience again.

'My last prizes today go to a very special team. Here at the Pony Palace, we have a rider and a horse who've stuck with each other through thick and thin. This prize is for Jamie Hall, who never gives up and never gives in.'

There's another big round of applause as Jamie squeezes and I walk forward. I'm really glad for him. He deserves this.

'And last, but definitely not least,' Kate adds, 'is my award to Jamie's partner, Rupert. Rupert, this prize is for you.'

She stops for a moment and it looks like there are tears in her eyes.

'Please accept this special award for long service to the riders of the Pony Palace,' she says. 'I know that you've been feeling tired for some time now, so today, Rupert, I am officially announcing your retirement.'

It takes a few moments for Kate's words to sink in. The adults are all standing now, clapping and cheering for me. I don't know whether to feel happy or sad. All the other ponies are snorting and whinnying and

congratulating me and I realise they've all been in on this all along. Kate places a ribbon around my neck and gives me a gentle kiss on the nose.

'I know you can be a bit grumpy some-times,' she says. 'But you've always come out to ride, rain, hail or snow – even when you didn't want to.'

She turns to the audience. 'Ladies and gentlemen, Rupert will be retiring from all riding lessons, but he'll still be living here at the Pony Palace and you're all welcome to come and visit him.'

Kate smiles at me and scratches me softly behind the ear.

'Jamie insisted that we celebrate your retirement like this, Rupert. He's your biggest fan and he's really going to miss riding with you. But you'll still be here and you'll still be loved and surrounded by all your friends. We're very lucky to have you, Rupert – and I hope you know how lucky *you* are to have had so many wonderful riders over the years.'

And do you know what? I absolutely do. Jamie parades me around the arena and the noise of applause and congratulations is deafening. I can see grown-ups who rode me when they were boys and girls many years ago, back when I was as young and spirited as Skippy. For some of them I was their very first pony.

I see Barney and Biscuit and Kaz and Tonto and Daisy and lots of the other horses who have shared this arena with me over the years. And as Jenny pulls the big door of the arena back, we all look outside and see the sun setting over the Pony Palace and I really have a lump in my throat. The stables and the arena are all bathed in a soft, pale light that twinkles on our coats. It's the perfect ending to a perfect day.

Our riders dismount and walk us to our

stables. Parsley is nickering softly to me and Skippy is telling me she hopes she will serve the Pony Palace for as long as I did. They tell me they've been keeping this a secret for weeks. I can't believe how lucky I am. I may be getting old and tired and grumpy, but I still have lots of wonderful friends here. Our riders are brimming with excitement about their own lives, too.

'I can't believe Dad came to see me! I'm so happy he's home!' Ben is saying.

Sophie seems to be on cloud nine too, telling the boys how her mum and dad are both going to come to lessons with her every week from now on.

Jamie is the quietest, and I know he's still a bit worried about his granddad. I think he's going to really miss me – and I know I'm going to miss him. I think he's been my favourite rider of all time at the Pony Palace.

We can smell the sweet, clean straw as we walk into the stables and as our bodies warm up, we whinny across to each other – Parsley, Skippy and me. We look out over the half door and watch the happy families leaving the Pony Palace together. I think about the lovely, long future ahead of me; relaxing and grazing and taking each day at my own pace, watching new kids and old kids come and go, keeping an eye on Kate and keeping the other ponies in line, and I know I couldn't be happier. Long live retirement and long live the Pony Palace!

The End

Fact Files

Name	Skippy
Colour	Grey
Height	13 hh
Loves	Cantering
Hates	Staying still

Name	Parsley
Colour	Chestnut
Height	12 hh
Loves	Looking pretty
Hates	Other ponies being too close to her bottom!

Name	Rupert
Colour	Chestnut
Height	12 hh
Loves	Relaxing in his stable
Hates	Working too hard

Acknowledgements

My thanks to Philippa, all the instructors, volunteers, parents and children at Lessans' for your fun and friendship over the past few years, and thank you to my family and friends for their support.

A special thank you to Mia Lewis for appearing on our front cover.

I am grateful to Ann and Tom at the Nosebag Cafe for their faith, food and friendship. Finally, a very, very big thank you to Damian Smyth and the Arts Council of Northern Ireland for their belief in me.

Also in the
Pony Friends Forever series

eBook
EPUB ISBN 978–0–85640–580–8
KINDLE ISBN 978–0–85640–598–3

Paperback
ISBN 978–0–85640–923–3

www.blackstaffpress.com